the *seasons* within her

Alankrutha M

First Edition: September 2024
Printed in India

Printed at: SAP Print Solutions Pvt. Ltd., Mumbai
Typeset in Adobe Garamond Pro

ISBN: 978-93-6070-888-7

Cover Design : Prajakta Sawant

Publisher: StoryMirror Infotech Pvt. Ltd.
                  Unit No-F/705, 7th Floor, Kailas Corporate Lounge,
                  Veer Savarkar Road, Vikhroli Park Site, Vikhroli West,
                  Mumbai-400079, Maharashtra, India.

Web: https://storymirror.com
Facebook: https://facebook.com/storymirror
Twitter: https://twitter.com/story_mirror
Instagram: https://instagram.com/storymirror
Email: marketing@storymirror.com

DEDICATION

This book is dedicated;
To Ram, my dad who has a heart of gold.
To Indu, my mum who is the bravest person I've ever known.
To, all my late grandparents. I hope you are looking after me from somewhere high above in the clouds. I hope this makes you proud.
To, Akanksha who never treated me anything less than her own sister.
To, Jeevitha, Sudip, and Divyashree
who have read and reviewed almost
every poem in this book;
The three people I would always go home to.

ACKNOWLEDGEMENTS

This endeavor could not have been possible without the humongous support from Storymirror Infotech. It has been a pleasure collaborating with a renowned organization that has helped many people publish their works.

I could not have undertaken this journey, without the guidance, reviews, and feedback from the editorial board and Mr. Abhishek Mishra, the Sales head who has generously provided me with knowledge and expertise.

I am also grateful to St. Claret Pre-university College which has played a very big role in encouraging me to write more than ever.

Thanks should go to all my classmates and cohort members who have been a great drive for me to compete. My teachers have always supported me through my highs and lows. Special thanks should go to my English professor, Mr. Tenzing Palyon, who has always been a mentor and an inspiration. His active role as a poetry enthusiast ignited my passion for poetry. I would like to extend my thanks to all those books of poetries that I've read that made me want to write one of my own. And, for research and knowledge, I looked up to libraries which should be thanked as well.

Lastly, I would be remiss in not mentioning my family. My dad has pushed me and encouraged me to publish my work. My ever-smiling mum, who is always proud of me and my biggest support. Thanks should go to Jeevitha, my first friend and best friend who has stuck with me since times immemorial.

This is for all of you.

And for all of me.

PREFACE

If I ever told ten-year-old me that in seventeen years of my life, I would know and realize that I was crafted for writing and perhaps would write a whole book consisting of words that I would never speak out loud, ten-year-old me would freak out. That is because talking out from the heart and communicating with someone never came to me as naturally as writing did.
On a random November night, when sleep wouldn't walk through the doors of my eyes, the theme and idea of this book was born.
The sole purpose of compiling "The Seasons Within Her" is derived from a lot of personal experiences. It is either things that I have been through or things that I have observed and witnessed. And at times, I had to let my imagination take part in it as well. To be a child who grew up in the bubble of loneliness, to be a girl who was nothing but a straight-A student and a "nerd", and to be a teen with no social media and little to no friends, I was somehow in a way lugged out of this by what I wrote.
This book deeply reflects one's emotions and experiences in the rawest form of poetry. Though poetry and a lot of literature include intricate versions that are hard to comprehend, I wanted to write simple things in a manner that would caress someone's thoughts or heart. And, being a teenager has brought in a whole bunch of unexplainable matters that I consider as lessons that life taught me.
I am grateful for the contribution and support of my family, friends, teachers, relatives, and publishing partners for making scribbled poetries in the last pages of random notebooks come to life as a book on its own.
The book is divided into four parts: winter, spring, summer, and autumn. The idea of each of these sections or seasons determines a phase of life that everyone goes through. Through each section, you will learn about suffering, loss, hope, happiness, and sacrifice. As we all are aware seasons usually start with spring and end with winter, it happens the other way around in this book for a reason.

A lot of times that needed research I always looked up to books and people that knew information better than me. I had a bunch of experts review my work as and when I progressed. Most of my research included brainstorming and exploration from the internet.

For the book to make sense, I would recommend the readers approach their emotional intelligence over logical one. Poetry is more than just sentences and words, it is someone's thoughts, someone's feelings, and at the end of the day, someone's life. Lastly, I couldn't have been happier if you have picked my book and given me a chance to let my work approach you. I am sure that there is more than one poem of mine, that you can relate to and feel in your veins.

My ten-year-old self would still not buy all this.

Contents

WINTER

When the cold air froze her cuticles, warms hearts, and hearths always radiated its heat and kept her alive all through, the lengthy, wintery nights.

1. PETUNIAS IN HER HAIR.

It was rather not peculiar;
her seasons started with winter.

Her petunias had shriveled their way away,
and found their home amidst the pages of her neatly bound
bookends.
Those unending pages scribbled with poetries
of love, valor, and death
pervaded her and kept her cozy.

Every time the winter air nipped her skin, she'd
ponder a little more
of a season she was chirpy in.
She did not hate the winters.
She despised it.

She wanted those vibrant petunias in her hair,
Not in her books, withered their way away.

On the first day of isolation,
she confined herself to infinite fantasies.
She put soapberries in her hair and
played a jigsaw puzzle on her own because
memories stuck to her heart with the strongest adhesive.

She cried in the bath,
then sat by the fireplace.
Her heart frosted
with bruises and numbness
which never seemed to
melt.

She swore the cold a thousand times.

And complained
that she couldn't sow a seed.
Before slumber slowly lulled her in,
on the first day of isolation,
she told herself that she was alive but did not intend to live.

The clouded sky,
with the moon affixed.
Beaming and cascading all its light down
on me, along
with the gyrating breeze.

Only to caress
sting
stab and
puncture, my day
to bring back those thoughts
which I can never seem to put away.
Everyone admires the creases of the moon
but,
what of me, now?
I too have creases at the edges
of my rarest smiles.
Am I not the same?

I don't have a light of my own.
Yet, I can channelize
ten thousand blazing suns
and brighten your paths,
on your darkest nights.

Don't take me for being imperfect;
rather know me
learn about me
and about the moon,

of how we are similar.
And one day you'll know
or rather realize,
that the beauty we see in the moon,
exists
in a person as well.

———•◆•———

4. THE AFTER LIFE.

A gloomy evening when a corpse took a stroll,
the streets had wilted
leaves stuck under the concrete.

So it walked till
feet calloused,
skin disheveled,
and hair became a wreck.
It walked, hoping to find a vineyard.
Instead, it ended up in a dense maze,
that was made of memories.

Frightened, it walked
a thousand miles to seek a different life.
Yet, it thought it never found one.

When the maze stomped it down,
the shins bloodied and
shoulders fought
with a dead heart,
heavier than any metal.

Before it realized,
the corpse was running.
Tearing the skin off its face,
decomposing again
into a crying mess.

As it neared the edge of the light,
at the sound of a loud conch,
it struggled to get back on its feet.

But it stood up
and ran because,
a new life was only
blinks away.
The sockets were out of
it's eyes,
blinding its vision.

The corpse sprinted now,
with all the might.
Before, it realized
the next time it
fell
it had a new
life.

A life that would
not remember
memories,
sadness,
suffering,
or breathing.
It wouldn't remember
a thing,
not even the slightest one
from the old lives.

———•❖•———

5. HOME.

How I love waking up to those mornings
when I hear cuckoos sing from the margins
of a place I'd never dare to enter again.

I love waking up on those mornings,
when I remember how
the walls of my bedroom engulfed me
in a nightmare last night.

Those mornings when
scorching hot water feels like nothing.
Those mornings when
pressing my clothes without having to burn myself becomes
a tedious task.

And finally, when I'm dressed, my mind asks me a
thousand times if,
I am tidy,
if, I am ready.
If, I am fine.

I love waking up on those mornings
when I lie to myself
push my exhausted body
to be in a place
that is not home.
And to lead a life
whose cause was long dead.

❖

6. POISON UNDER THE SEA.

A soul was wandering free,
it lived on its own just like a tree.
And there came another soul to see,
so into its arm, it did flee.
Oh! it's such a shame that it turned out
to be the poison under
the beautiful sea.

7. SUNSHINE TO SILVER.

If she were rays of sunshine,
their bloodshot eyes were thorny pine.
They stabbed and slayed her with words
until it scarred her nerves.

She sowed a seed in them, anticipating a harvest,
She had nothing but a pest.
Brown orbs walloped raven ones,
making them feel like a ton of sun.
They said they'd stay,
throughout the day.

But when darkness clasped her,
they shone as if they were silver.
As they absorbed all her light.
They secluded her by the night.

8. PLATONIC?

She could write a whole book about the silent
and a cryptic conversation they had with their eyes.

Their silence sang a new tune,
a melody, and a rhythm with which they both bonded.
Their looks wrote new letters
with indelible ink.

Caressing each other without touching,
they lay awake when the moonlight poured
and nuzzled under their skins.

A gust of wind stroked against his fingertips.
Those rigid fingers she always longed to hold.
There he was,
on the other end,
always ruminating about the stories she told.

9. SLUMBERLESS NIGHTS.

I see it every day, everywhere perhaps.
Mouthful of food, rheumy eyes drooping, causing no
mishaps.

I still ponder why it might be different,
eating and sleeping are resentment.

Golden, hazel, raven, and auburn orbs lit up at the sight of
delicacies.
I wish nausea didn't invade me as I glanced at these
intricacies.

Black skies and cold nights,
They prick my skin like termites.

'Sleep well', they say,
Head shakes and tired eyes obey.

But what they never know,
Or something that I'd never show is
that Slumber isn't a friend of mine.
It left me alone amongst the stars,
And yes it is a crime.

❖

10. DEAD FLOWERS.

A pair of pale hands
with tears glistening in her eyes,
points to
her tiny flower pot on the
porch outside.

"My flower died," she hiccups
while sorrow clouds her flushed
cheeks and,
the corners of her lips lie low.

"Come here," beckons a hand that is
jaggy and peeled.
Her mother sits her down
while she soothes her sobbing away.

"I hate winters," she says, sniffling.
"And why is that?" asks mum.
"Because my flowers died," she blames.

A familiar smile creeps up her mother's face
and she explains,
that flowers suffer and die in the cold
only
to bloom in the spring
only
to be celebrated in the summer
only
to be left with the memory of it in the autumn.

14... *Alankrutha M*

"It is a cycle and everyone goes through it," Mum assures.
"So, are we also dead flowers sometimes?" she asks with doe eyes.
Amidst her soft chuckling Mother says, "Yes baby, you are right".

⸻⸱◈⸱⸻

Rays of sunshine intruded on our love.
Yet, we fought a battle in the blue sky.
The blue faded away,
and we painted the sky grey
just as we walked away.

12. DEVIOUS.

When life became devoid,
she became devious.
Life threw obstacles at her,
but she rolled her eyes.

Or perhaps when life gambled with her fears;
she stood in melancholy and suited herself to solitude.
"It will all be fine," Mum always assured her.
Oh, but life cackled and called her mum wrong.

Life never made her furious.
It made her give up on everything,
which was worse than anything.

13. HE IS WHO HE IS.

It was just a small thread-like thought.
When I thought it through,
it indeed unveiled.

He is who he is,
because of the people he went home
with and for.

He is who he is
because there were a pair of gentle hands
feeding him supper.
And there were those hands that patted his back.
He remains who he is,
maybe because of a lost friend,
who he'd never stop reminiscing.

He is who he is because of
A boy who is a brother to
him like no other.
He is who he is because,
seasons fall apart as they grow
but, a crowd of his three friends is
his family that he will never show.

He is who he is,
but, I wonder
How bewitched one made him
as he sketched that beautiful face,
onto his parchment.

18... *Alankrutha M*

He is who he is,
because each of them
Did thread, knit, stitch, and weave,
A beautiful cloth.
And wrapped him in the same fabric of silk,
to trust him as a present.
My heart takes a thousand vows.
To keep it safe and loved.

He is who he is,
because of the people he went home with and for.
He is who he is;
because he became home
to a girl who didn't have one.

As the cold grew, she fought it less.
Her reflexes became stronger by the night.
The melted wax from her candles hardened up.

Cold crawled up to her.
It made her bones
brittle
and eyes
bloodshot.

Yet, the song of cricket became a melody for her.
Slowly, she smiled when the
clouds conquered the sun.
Little by little, she never wanted to meet the cold like
how the shadow never met reflection.

But, she pondered
if she is acquainted with the cold
or had embraced it
and became
the cold herself.

---

15. BREATHE.

Learn to breathe by love.
Learn to breathe by family.
By friends, by acquaintances.
Learn to breathe with a hug.
Or a kiss, perhaps.
Breathe for your pet
and for your perils.

But how is that?
Some learn it the harder way.

They freeze to death
to know the first breath.
They bloom in life
to learn the fresh breath.
They tan like summer itself
to know the hot breath.

And finally
they fall like autumn leaves
to grounds underneath,
dark and muddy, like those of
the nightmares
where there is no air
and they struggle to breathe.

While some,
drown.
In the deepest of those blue oceans,

where new fears are born.
They drown only
to learn
how to breathe.

————◆◆◆————

22... *Alankrutha M*

16. THE BIRTHDAY STORY.

She roused to the song of screeching peacocks.
A chorus of "Happy Birthday" sung
by her mum,
which popped the dimple on her chin.

On that day, of a rather gloomy November,
she ran with the greyish clouds,
filled her shelves with new hard bounds
and felt a little less lonely.

She endured the birthdays
like she endured the cold.

But for that day,
her mind slipped off from the winter and dashed to
the core of leisure.

She gobbled up ice cream
and danced outside in the fog.
"I want to love the cold on my next birthday.,"
she made a wish and blew
her candles.

17. THE FIRST RAIN.

It was another day when
he sat there in a park ingrained
in the rhythm of swallows.

I saw him from afar,
mourning over a creased
piece of yellowish paper.
It tumbled out of his hand and
flowed all around the place
as he walked away.

My pale hands picked it up gently,
And scanned the cursive script.
"I will wait for you," it said.
With an address on the back.

But, I remember
his face oozed despair
like a hobby.
I had seen him before,
he was
a jaw clenched.
With an overcoat that
hung along with his sadness.
He had the face,
of a harsh winter
with grey hailstorms,
for his eyes.
And lips pursed as if

he was a soul, wandering
at a loss for words.

So I walked away too.
And on the next day,
while I sat in the same park
looking for
a love that was lost
high above in the skies.

He came and took
his seat in front of me.
I peeked at him
while I was scribbling on my sheets.
He sat there,
completely numb.
A face,
devoid of emotions
staring at the sky,
hoping for a miracle.

A heavy rush of wind;
blew my papers to his face.
And I ran,
with my heart
out on my sleeve.
He peeled those papers
off his face,
while I stood before him.

My brown eyes of the ground
struck the grey ones of his clouds.
Thunder roared in a couple of seconds.

Down came the rain
so dark and full.
If he were the clouds,
I was the ground.
When our eyes met
so did our worlds'.

He spilled his tears
and
I absorbed him.
As we melted into each other,
We made
the scent of rain smother.

— ❖ —

18. CRANES AND CHANGE.

A colony of cranes
flows past the seeping,
rays of sunshine, with
the towering skyscrapers underneath.

Their ivory bodies blending,
into that cloudy sky.
The mother calls to
her child,
loudly rattles,
and the child follows.
So that,
he doesn't get lost
in the widest skies.

They all fly,
in harmony and
in hope.
To find a finer place.
A place,
they would call their home.

Their shrieks beckoning to one another
telling to never settle for anything less.
They fly and fly,
in search of a season
that brings them solace.

They fly as if their
wings have a fuel that
does not give up.
Cranes try hard
very hard, perhaps
for a change.

They fly during the brightest days
and sometimes on the darkest nights.
The mother still calls to her child,
and he follows her
because he knows,
that they fly
for a change, a better one.

And seasons are the changes
that they must
adapt,
love,
experience,
and live a life with.

SPRING

It was a season she went home to.
Her favorite flowers bloomed.
So did her saccharine fruits.
She loved the spring,
because it shed some light.
Lights that she never emitted.
It added colors to her life.
Colors she never possessed.

1. SHE WAITS.

When the sun torches the grubby earth,
she waits.
Even when rain drums on her roof
or floods her favorite garden,
she waits.

She waits for birds to fly.
And for the flowers to knock on her door.
She waits, like
a quiet life hidden
from the naked eye.
She waits,
till exhaustion dances
from inside out.

While she waits till
she absorbs the most
minuscule bit of hope
and ray of sunshine.

As she knew that waiting
will always bring her
new presents.
A back lawn with a lush green cover,
a house that becomes a home,
a father who,
will grow flowers
for the mother, and
a family that remains intact like no other.

And sometimes
just sometimes,
she wonders
if she waits to
love this season
or loves to wait
for this season.

2. HE CLUTCHED THOSE FLOWERS.

As the wind whistled,
Pale streaks of mauve adorned the evening skies.
The fields garnished
with vibrant flower heads,
while his sighs danced to the
chiming of the church bells.

On that evening, of a rather blossoming spring,
his fist firmly held a bouquet of paperwhites.
He strolled through the wilderness and
The downtown road,
blazed by thousands of summers
and frozen by thousands of winters.

While he walked,
he thought a little more
of how dyes and flowers had changed with time.

His blossoms and hues were impeccable, but,
lives were not.
He was the boy who dunked his brushes
and dyed the seasons of solace.
But the vibrant days were long gone
and embers remained.

'Flowers for your wife, eh?' chuckled,
the old man in the alleyway.

He pressed his lips into a thin line,
as curt nods had his back.

If only they knew that the flowers clutched,
graced cemeteries as well.
He placed those paperwhites,
on the grave and
sighed more, as he told himself that
he had painted a world
that was not meant for him
to live in.

And all that was vibrant was now grey.

———•◈•———

3. A SPIRIT THAT COULD MOVE MOUNTAINS.

As the sky inked itself raven,
I caught a glimpse of her slouched back,
Deep dark bags under her eyes had taken.

There was something about the way she'd try,
scribbling onto her parchment
and nibbling on her skin.
She'd sigh for what felt like the hundredth time
but never cry.

Yet how amusing it was, she'd smile.
The crinkles formed at the sides of her temples.
I want to travel with her, take her out,
and sit by the river Nile.

Her aura was wild.
For wild, like the jungles,
which dangled with adventure
and crept scruples up your skin.

Sometimes she'd tell me
how hard things were.
Gripping her pale palms
I'd listen to her deeply.

I'd tell her not to give up
because that is not her.
She deserves to be wrapped
in a quilt and kept warmly.

'A hug' would be the medicine
when she is exhausted.
I am aware she'd get her fruits
for working this hard.
I'd wipe those tears
while she lamented.

And take her to walk in a vineyard.
I would tell her that she
has a spirit that'd move mountains.
So that she'd never mistake
herself for sobbing fountains.

⁕

4. WORDS.

I could certainly say,
that my words told everything I felt.
It came from the roots of my heart,
where the ground
was damp and cold.

Those words
that I told
or rather wrote
begged for you to notice
how my shackled hands couldn't
reach for help.

My words became prayers soon
because I became
a stranger in my skin.
And in times, the words
others said
became far more salient.
For some words
never failed to crawl under my bones.
They pricked my heart with
the sharpest needles.

Words are the strong sort,
because, your harshest words
were the most beautiful
pieces of my poetry.

I do have a way with the words I write
because,
the voice chords of my throat
were twisted and tangled nastily,
by a set of other mean words.

There were definitely
millions of words,
but
my words flowed
along with the
red hollies,
the sweet tulips,
the mangoes,
and the fallen oak leaves.

⁎

5. AN EFFORTLESS SLEEP.

Slowly, putting the
baggage of winter off her shoulders
she stands there in the radiant sun,
waiting for the rays
to reach the coldest parts
to melt away.

She waters all her flowers
that day,
hoping that their blooming
will make her smile.
She leaves the cattle to graze,
and feeds the birds
their favorite meal of the day.

The cluster of golden dust
she has for eyes,
wanders into the bluest skies,
and searches for
shapes in the clouds.

She puts flowers in her hair,
sweeps her skirt all over the place,
and dances for the dusk
to take over.

While she had a lovely day,
she recalls of
how going to sleep
a few months back
was exhausting
from blood and bones.

But, now
a spontaneity builds and
when she sleeps,
she doesn't just sleep.
Rather, she smiles in her sleep.

———•❖•———

6. THREE IS ONE.

Or perhaps it was a story
about three friends,
who built a home in each other's heart?

It started with her and him, and
soon after I blended into them.
Three became one,
and we reckoned it would last more than this entity

But what of it now?
Ask those eye bags under her eyes.
Ask my hands that are peeled off their last shred of skin.
Yet, he nibbled on the minute bit of a bad memory.

What is it to him?
We were everything to him,
once.
We are not anything to him,
now.

Three became two.
She left, as she sought her priorities
I stayed.
For he was not a choice,
but the only option.
Was it all just words spewed?
Those times when we spoke of how her children
would be the god-children of mine and his.

It pained me to say,
that if I threw a stone into
A pond called 'our friendship'.
Ripples would form showcasing our memories.

Had I known,
Those memories were all I'd get with them,
I'd have dared not to cross their path at all.
Tell me this distance is temporary.
Tell me,
we three are one.

———•◈•———

7. GUARDIANS OF THE SEA.

When you plunge into the wilderness,
Rippling through the saline water,
Hear the sounds of the tide through the unending peace.

When you pass through these swamps of mangrove
You comprehend the bond between
these dense tangles of roots and the brine.

The roots are clusters of unity,
Endlessly getting indulged in the seawater.
Amidst the serene tranquil
you can discover,
The snap of the twigs of the guardians of the sea.

Yet you see them standing as if they were on silt,
But it all paves down to the roots

As they behold one another with the utmost union,
They sure form a coalition
with the foaming salt water
striving to survive.

❖

8. QUIET LIVES.

I once knew quiet lives,
camouflaged deep down the shreds
of their bodies.

I often saw them,
wondered "That's me too,"
because quiet lives
were difficult to live with.

Our minds had made up
monologues that our
mouths couldn't spit.
It's true, our lives
concealed far behind
in the thickest shrub you
could ever find.

I once knew quiet lives.
The smallest things
caused their biggest grins.

Even though trauma zipped
their mouths
shut it tight, and
glued them.
They could still say words
that made someone
else's day.

44... *Alankrutha M*

Quiet lives hide under the
lashes of your eyes,
for you to sense
the
narrow distance between
them and the others.
The thin roads
that they saunter on.
The darkest memories that
cloud their whole life.

I had a quiet life, too.
I read my way through everything,
and learned about
the world with my nose
buried in the pages of age-old books.
I listened to instrumentals,
with no lyrics
so that I could fuel my
imagination to write
my own words to them.
I sat alone in parks admiring nature.
Once in a while,
I'd catch up with that
one friend who never stopped being
mine.

I knew quiet lives,
veiled away from certain eyes.
because,
those eyes never meant
to see the beauty of solitude.

I knew a lot of quiet lives,
because
I had a quiet life, too.

<hr>

9. EARTH HEALS ITSELF.

Pick up an encyclopedia
and start scanning through a
hundred-something pages of the thickest book.

Read about Mother Earth and
the greatest ballad of her healing.
Recall the times,
she had held Pangea together
and it split.
But she built new homes
with blossoming hopes;
conquering her.

You do recall, don't you?
Her biggest wave that
took people's lives
became the frothy water
that our kids played in.

She had droughts but
also an oasis.
She had humongous volcanoes,
spitting the fires of her rage.
Yet, she had those lush green
ranges of valleys and mountains
that never seemed to end.

Man did everything.
To make her
filthy.
To make her
loose.
To squeeze the life
out of her.

Still, she heals
and her story remains flowing
in front of our naked eyes
every day to prove
that her every wound and
every gash heals
with time,
with seasons,
with a small amount of people who care
for her.

Perhaps, when you read
or when you witness
you will understand
that she is the
teacher
who teaches
that being hurt
would lead to the art of healing.

———•❖•———

48... *Alankrutha M*

10. THE TALE OF TWO BEST FRIENDS.

A crimson blouse, with a sneer
plastered on her face.
She greeted me as if she held
a grudge against me.
Her conjoined dark brows,
pulled up
conveyed that she was going through a phase.

She left me locked in the loo on my first day.
We fought wars through our eyes.
But, tables turned once, and I called her Ray.
She was a ray of sunshine
and tired eyes with bags.
She went vulnerable with me.
I found traces of solace
or perhaps home, as we
entwined hands.

Inseparable was a word, probably.
I love how we became an example of it.
One day you showed up and told
your knees felt wobbly.
I noticed the purple bruises with a swollen eye
and you slightly slurred.

Heart shatteringly, you cried to me.
I held you tight, embraced you tighter.

Until your tears softened into toothy grins.
Soon she was laughing while we played frisbee.
She always told me "No one could get under our skins,"

Those were the days when she
gobbled up my lunches
and fed her lunches to my dog.
Those were the days when she wrote,
greetings to me in bunches.
And laughed when we found a shoe with a frog.

I will hold her close
until I write about her.
I will hold her close,
till she paints my life with
the happiest hue.

One day, after many years.
When they grow big enough to comprehend.
I will tell her children with tears,
the tale of two best friends that never did end.

11. YELLOW LOVE.

Tulip lost the hope of finding new love.
There are a thousand different rows
of colors,
from the same earth
where she blooms.

But,
far in the distance,
a familiar
vibrant shade catches her eye.
It is a shade,
that paints the rays in the skies.
It is the color of the sun itself.

Far in the distance,
tulip
sees
the brightest shade
of yellow,
with a thousand velvety petals,
and a face as brown as
the ground.

He stands there,
saluting the sun.
Soon,
tulip waves from her home
to his.

She notices him smiling
with a face,
radiant than that
of the sun.

The world
thought that the sunflower was way too bright.
What is it to her if the world thought so?
Perhaps her world knows that
he still makes her feel
loved
from afar.

And when spring is here
colors are all over the place.
She celebrates
her season with
great pomp and show.

Tulip grows bigger bulbs,
she sings the other flower heads
a love lullaby.

And even though,
sunflower faces towards
the sun,
he dances to her new tune,
with his stalk
swinging and
head swirling.

Rarely, he glance at her
and when he does,
he always shouts
out to her.

For her
he wasn't a flower,
he was home.
A home grounds away
that kept her roots intact
and her flowers blooming.

Tulip makes sure that he
is dancing ever so happily
on each sunrise.
While sunflower
secretly promises
all of his sunsets with her.

12. PEN AND PAPER.

It is mundane,
when I imagine what
would I have possibly done
if pen and paper
never fostered me like their child.

I had different
pens put up
on my pen stand.
Yet, I would choose the one
pen which I clicked a thousand times
to get new ideas.
I swirled it between my fingers,
bobbed the cap
to write two lines of my poetry.

While my pen was patient
my parchment,
hoped I would
write the most beautiful
lines on her that day.
Sometimes, I did
and sometimes I didn't.
But they never lost faith in me.

When I was a head
full of thoughts
and anguish,
I picked up the pen,

held the parchment
and started writing.

I wrote poetries, as
prayers to save strangers' lives.
I wrote stories,
that would twist the pages of
history itself.
I wrote letters,
addressed to no one
and stuck stamps.
I wrote scripts,
to know if I held
the strength to
be someone's voice.
And for those notes of
music,
I wrote lyrics like
it gave meaning to my
own life.

When I had pen and paper,
the power
in my hand
was unfathomable.

I was a nobody
who was
afraid to see
her reflection
on the windows of the subway,
took the lone staircase,

and traced my hand along the
dust from the railings.

But,
when I vented out my sadness
to my blue ink
and my white paper
they always listened.

They made me write words.
Words that,
I thought I never knew.
And soon,
pen and paper became my home.
The paper
became a thatched roof
over my sadness, that rained
and the pen withheld the paper with
all might,
so that I could have shelter.

It is mundane,
when I imagine what
would I have possibly done
without my pen and paper
because, before
I saw the world
for what it was.
And now
they made me see the world
for what it could be.

——◈——

56... *Alankrutha M*

13. A TINY LITTLE MUSING.

A tiny little musing
knocks the back of her brain as
she lays her head against the windowpane.
Her fingers tapping and tuning,
with the drumming rain.

A tiny little musing of a beautiful life
affixes her as
a small grin creeps up her lips.

A tiny little musing,
of how she thinks that
seasons exist within her
as if she is every beautiful fragment
of the universe, put together.

A tiny little musing
of how spring kisses her knuckles,
when they go pale.

A tiny little musing
of how there are millions
of roads in life,
yet she walks on something
harsh
but loved.

A tiny little musing,
of her growing old next to a person
with wrinkles on her face
making her look as beautiful as ever.

A tiny little musing of holding
the heaviest books that would
take her to the world's unknown.

A tiny little musing,
of making her favorite tea
and filling it up to the brim
of her ivory cups.

Just a tiny little musing,
as she sits on the patio
of her house and wonders,
of how it was a sign of the
universe itself
that paved the way for
her to lead this
life.

—•❖•—

14. FAVORITES.

For most of the time,
I never realized
how when someone asked me
about my favorites
my throat would go
parched,
my eyes blinked more than it
should, and
as for my voice never made it
out of my glands.

I would stand there
in dismay, like
a rotten flower
with head bent
and I shrugged.

I shrugged because
I didn't know
what my favorites were.

There were surely
a dozen things I'd do
with my heart
and soul put into.
But,
why does one need to weigh
them as favorites?
Perhaps it was because

someone out there,
were at peace with
something that they liked.
Something that they liked,
a bit more than the rest of the lot.

Slowly, I understood
that it is okay
to not have a favorite song,
or a favorite meal,
or a favorite book,
or a favorite person.

As favorites
were only a matter
of choices
but not the only
option.

Slowly, I also understood
that even though
I have never had favorites,
I had a desire that burned
from every cell of mine
to be
someone's favorite.

When I recalled
those weary smiles,
of certain memories
I could surely picture
you as someone
who wore a clear glass frame,
made fun of your nose,
told me
that my smile was the most
precious thing
and stuttered for
words like they
were not your strong suit.

I wish I knew the day
we spoke, that
you would be
the greatest lesson
of
how
to
loose
a
friend.

A piece of my heart
was left behind

in those words
I wrote to you.

A new friend was
always a good sign
and I thought so too.

I remember how distance,
barged into a person
I went home to.

Priorities were the key,
but we locked
the doors of our hearts
and shut the windows of
our brains so tight that
unspoken words
or emotions couldn't
find a shelter.

When I thought back on things,
I could see
that you had grown
into a beautiful human
but evolved into a stale mind.

Hurtful things were
the sharpest nails
that dug into
my brain
and punctured
the bond we had.

Still, I made it out of
there.
While you recovered
from something that I said.

And we tried again.
Each time we tried,
I believed
a little less
and a little less
that mending
two hearts
that were bruised,
consumed my patience
like it was a fuel.
Ate me up alive,
like I was the fodder.

By the days' food
seemed like worms
that would harm me.
And by the nights
sleep never
listened to my cries.

Shards of glass were
buried deep into my
bloody knuckles when
I begged
for this to end.

And somewhere
at the back of my brain,

where I am engulfed
in the conversations we had
and the time spent.

I still wished
your happiness
over piano notes,
and passions.

I felt like a thousand
daggers latched onto me
when I wrote about you
in the past tense.

Your tongue-tied
shrugs, and smiles
was the best memory.
A memory that would
haunt me
for the rest of my life.

Yet, a memory that would
tell me the story
of a long-lost friend.

———•◈•———

16. LONELY LANE.

While the rest of the
world knew what
to do.
Somewhere at the end
of the street
where the road met the lawn,
there would be someone
who swerved into
the lane of loneliness,
lost
in the lunacy of dreams.

Rotten under pressure
of what success looked like,
chaos invaded and made
them count the
number of times they breathed.

While the rest of the world
defined dreams that would
lead to success.
The people on the Lonely Lane,
extinguished the ego
of the others
that torched their brains
and burned their hearts.

While the rest of
the world called it "indecisiveness"

faltered smiles and legs
that limped on the lonely lane
begged the dreams
of their own to be
a considerable friend.

But,
the world needed
successful people,
who flourished in
money and status.
Nobody needed
people
who were happy.

Sanity taught that
happiness was the home
of people who
got lost in the Lonely Lane.

Yet, nobody there
was a life
that was devoid of
hope.
They shoveled their
way through
the harshest snowstorm
of success.

The Lonely Lane
watered the seeds
of happiness
which bloomed into

66... *Alankrutha M*

flowers that
welcomed the spring.

While the rest of the
world drowned in
the biggest ocean of
remorse and guilt.

The people
of the Lonely Lane
walked together.

The Lonely Lane left their age-old
footprints of failures
walked on the grass,
with bare feet.
Their hands,
intertwined
with the flowers of
the happiness they grew.

They walked
with a head held high,
and a soul that danced
with success itself.

17. DIAMONDS AND POETRY.

The way how pressure
deep down the surface of the
Earth,
melted the rigid raven
rocks into those
diamonds that never lost
it's luster.

The same way,
my heart held a
warehouse of
pain and pressure that
slowly,
melted into letters and
then into words
of wisdom.

And throughout
the harshest times,
I harnessed poetry
that shone
as bright as diamonds.

18. WHAT LOVE LOOKED LIKE.

I might have been young
but I was very much aware
that
love was nothing but
two people
who lived a decent life.

Love was two people
who had a garden that grew
their favorite variety
of hibiscus and sweetest
Of the mangoes.

Love was nothing but
two people
who raised not only
my mother
but also me
with the gentlest pair of
hands and
the purest smiles
any face could ever have.

When I was a little girl
love looked like
those faintest memories
that I held of

my grandma sitting in
her pale-colored saree with glasses
on the bridge of her nose
reading the thickest book
she could ever find.

Love looked like
those times when my
grandparents were ready
with cotton candies
in their hands, as
and when I came home from school.

Love indeed looked like
two people
who filled
a void in my heart
that my parents could never
because they were
hardly around.

Love looked like
two people
who stood with me
even when nothingness
cackled at them.

As and when
seasons fell apart,
I grew old enough
to realise
that love looked
like

70... *Alankrutha M*

my grandparents
who were like
a song stuck in my mind,
a haven where I cannot go anymore,
a season of spring which
was only alive
in those trees
they planted
in me.

SUMMER

Out of all the seasons she contained within, summer never
failed to make her skin gleam with happiness.
A light radiated from the corners of her cold heart.
Soon enough, the warm weather held her hand gently, took
her on a stroll, and made her realize the riot of emotions
inside of her.

1. SUMMER LOVE.

Summer love is
old hardbound and tired eyes
lost on the beach days.
Summer love is
messy hair, vampire teeth
and record players.

Summer love is
grimy old libraries and that
fragrance before it rains.
Summer love is
sappy old romance movies,
moments captured on disposables.

Summer love is
flowers, fruit-filled orchards
and classical music.
Summer love is
narrating stories
and poetries amidst the
western skies.

Summer love is
brownie-filled donuts and
bear hugs.
Summer love is
long scribbled letters.

Summer love
beckons me by a different name
the world isn't aware of.
Summer love is
everything
lovely,
lovelier
or perhaps
loveliest.

———◆※◆———

76... *Alankrutha M*

2. BEAUTIFUL BROWN GIRL.

Beautiful brown girl,
Your skin isn't just a color.
You're bathed in honey,
which never halts from being glazed.
Don't let their taunts and fuss bother you,
For you are the same earthy ground where gold is found.

Beautiful brown girl,
never blame yourself or your body.
It's the veiled eyes that cannot fathom your beauty.
You are the seeds of coffee ground and knead all over.
You are the epitome of energy or exquisiteness.

Beautiful brown girl,
You are everywhere in the nature.
You are the bronze roof
that soaks up the thumping rain.
You are the bark of the tree
home to the woodpecker.

Beautiful brown girl,
You are the very molecule of Mother Earth
blended and cast into a human,
who has a heart as beautiful
as her skin.

3. OF LIBRARIES AND LOVE.

The scent of bygone hardbound,

hit my nose

as I clutched that one book in my hand close.

I ran my fingers through the spine of the book,

whose plots often had me shook.

There stood a peculiar one,

which weighed a ton.

Scruples got the better of me,

making the enormous book the only thing I see.

Grabbing it off the wooden shelf,

I calmed my curious self.

As I flipped the yellow crinkly pages,

I reckon I found traces

Of poetry, of perils.

A withered violet stuck to a page

as if it was locked in a cage.

Gently putting away the violet,

I noticed the ink imprinted in Scarlett.

"You were the poem I've always wanted to write;
But all I did with you was fight.
Forgive me with all your might.
Promise me to fall in love at our next sight."

I snapped the book close.
Let my heart loose.
As I didn't want to go back to a truce.

⎯⎯⎯❖⎯⎯⎯

I hope it doesn't take much
to know that a lot
of liberation comes from the
brooding
that life belongs
to the whole
of you,
before
it becomes someone else's.

If one wonders,
a tad bit more
perhaps
they may understand that
someone's freedom
is not just an
entitlement
to roam without
barriers.

Rather,
it is an act of exploring
the vast adventures within
that struggle to
breathe
because
the living cells

of freedom
had walls
that are
thin
and veined
or perhaps caged.

A lot of liberation
teaches
that
to push,
is to push yourself,
but not push others down.
While to pull
is to pull your dreams,
not to pull away.

Freedom has
its own dictionary.
For some see freedom
as
heaven and beyond.
And for some,
Heaven or freedom is
just a fair-sized building
built with their favorite
things,
and brought to life
with their favorite people.

A lot of liberation is
found,
when loneliness becomes solitude,

when scars become strength, and
when summer becomes home.

A lot of liberation
comes from the idea
of
knowing
what
you
need is
far more important
from knowing
what you want.

———◦❖◦———

5. CIRCLES.

It is rather amusing how,
they are aware of the words
she carved on the board
but never do they ponder about
the dust that plummets down from her chalk.

How do they not know?
she picks up the pieces they left;
mend them and sieve their misery away.

Are they aware?
they see this world because of her;
"You know nothing, mum," they'd still say.

How could they do that?
Make her do too much labor
until she wore herself out.

For she is like a lamp;
she put herself to flames to emit light.

Her love is like a circle
it only has a beginning
and not an end.
She will kill for you
or rather die
all in a circle
and in the end,
she always comes home to you.

6. ROUTINES AND HAIRKNOTS.

A sudden burst of adrenaline
rushes
as she sees
specks of golden dust
dancing in the
morning rays.

She sits on the
edge of the window pane
scrutinizing,
with a warm smile
on her face,
with a warm scent
in the air, and
with a warm feeling
in her heart.

And that day,
putting painful
memories behind
she ties her hair
up in a knot
for the first time
in months,
because it was getting

heavy.
No.
It was getting sweaty.

Hair still in a bun,
she cleans her house
under the stairs,
under the choir rugs,
the chandeliers,
and the tapestries.
She
rubs them off
of their last bit of
debris.

She sighs because of the
heat but ate mangoes
and ice creams
like they were the only
meal.

When all of this
feels very routine,
for the first time
in months
she stands before
the mirror
and examines
her tan painted skin,
Golden
that outlines around
her pupil

she could
see her lips
curved
in a way
that
looked like
a smile.
All this while
she still had her hair
up in a knot.

7. TEARY CONVOS.

'How do you love father?' I asked.
Her glittery eyes and golden smile
made their way.
She left a contended sigh
and patted my head and said,

'It breaks all the weight of measures
and heights.
I love him like how the water
loves memory.
The memory of serving,
saving, or causing a peril.

I love him enough to
feel it in me;
in my every cell or
every molecule around.

I love him like how the raindrop loves the
sight of a ray of light;
which expects to form a rainbow.

I love him like how I love
the home above the skies
or the hell below the earth.

I love him much enough that in my memoir
every word I ink
on every page
would be a love letter to him.'

8. BLISS BECKONED.

For the first time
or perhaps
for the last
bliss came and called
my name out that day.

It was not a shout.
It was just a very
feeble whisper,
that flowed with the
summer wind,
tickled the
strands of my hair
and knocked
my eardrums.

When bliss beckoned
me
my droopy eyes shot up,
my nose smelled those
freshly bloomed marigolds, and
my lips hummed
a forgotten tune.
As for my hands
swerved to
the sun.

It was yet
just a whisper,

88... *Alankrutha M*

that played
hide and seek
between
my earlobes.

But,
the flowing
of hushed words
became
sounds that carried
waves thrown at my
feet.

Before I realized this,
I stood
there in front
of a whole ocean.
With foaming
water, bobbing
close to my legs, and
sand struck between
the corners
of my toenails.

The whisper
buzzed in my ears,
like a bee
and told me that
I would go down.

And I did.

My feet sank deeper into the sand,

stuck under the sticky
mud,
an enormous wave
elbowed me
into the water.

I couldn't swim.
I never knew how to,
or
maybe
I didn't want to swim.

When I drowned,
I saw blue for the
first time,
in a long time.
My nose struggled
because I couldn't
breathe
until pushed down.
My mouth wanted to
cry for help,
for the first time
because I never did
when I (was) fine.
Salt filled my lungs
while
my feet, hands
kicked and moved
for the first time,
as they were
exhausted of a war
with no motion.

90... *Alankrutha M*

The more I drowned,
the more I realized,
that
death was only minutes away
but,
I was not ready
to give up.
Not yet.

I caught a glimpse
of the sun
trying to
seep through
the blue
to reach the ocean floor.

And now,
the whisper
became a loud prayer,
that shot my hands up,
and
kicked my feet
to swim.

And I swam.

Washed
to the sand bed,
my hair
dripped thousand
tears,
the whisper
cheekily

approached me,
and said, "You swam".

For the first time
or perhaps for the last
bliss came and called
out my name that day,
because
it knew
that to breathe
and to swim
was a bliss that
I had to learn.

———◦❖◦———

9. WHAT I ADMIRE.

It didn't amuse me until
I grew old enough
to realize,
that, the love of my mum and dad
was not something I'd jot into a mere paper.
But, rather admire it from afar
how I was an integral part of their souls.

For I am the smile on my mother's face.
And the notes of music to those
tracks composed by my father.
I still admire,
how their work was their
was their first child.

I always admire how
My mum lent me her kindness.
While my father garnished his discipline on me.
I never fail to admire;
How they nurtured me to the person I am,
Even though they lived away from each other.

Perhaps the older I got
the more I perceived,
that they were two
different people
living two different lives.
But,
the sole reason

they lived for
was me.

I will continue to admire;
that the love of my parents
is not about how much they show.
But,
it is rather about
how much they sacrifice.

94... *Alankrutha M*

It sure was a bond like that
of the shore and the sea.

You'd find miniature
conchs buried in her.
And she'd let those
sandcastles of strangers
standstill.
She was the shore.

You'd find ships trying to
thrive in their way through him.
And he'd let those poisonous roots
have their home beneath a torbernite.
He was the sea.

There was a time when the sea embraced
the shore and kissed her gently.
There yet was a time when
they nuzzled into each other.

But,
soon after
he took her by an enormous

brackish wave.
And washed her away.
Not only her,
but,
their love, too.

11. GOLDEN.

Sweat beaded
on the sides of her
temples
as she walked,
with bulky bags
tucked under her
arms, which
strained the living
life out of her.

The sight of the bus
shudders and rash drivers
took over her (not) peaceful
evening,
that eventually led
her to the lake.

There was something
about the way,
the water danced
in the dazzling sun.
it was like
opposites wanting
to fall in love.

While she sat
enveloped in a silence
that shouted louder than

her insecurities,
she observed.

It was one of the
things that eased
the exhaustion that
remained.

When she felt grey,
amidst all the blues
and the greens
she saw colors in
faces of others,
shifting hands
that long to hold
each other, and
sweet bickering of
people in love.

She saw colors,
that they probably
couldn't see.
Not for themselves.

As the sun went,
down
when the warmth
of yellow was all over,
she noticed hands
running through a beloved's
hair,
hands begging for a
beloved to stay, and

98... *Alankrutha M*

hands around one's
torso mouthing
a hundred promises
to never leave.

It was a very foreign feeling
to her.

And even when,
she never knew
a single letter of
their names,
or what was the reason
behind their cheeky
smiles,
she easily
observed
and fused them
into brightest of the
colors.

And somewhere
when the time was up,
she bid her silent
prayers to the lake
and she pushed herself
to get up.

It was ironic
how she hadn't realised
that the
rays of the sun
had painted everyone

yellow,
but
she was
drenched in
a shade of
Golden,
that others
observed.
They saw the golden
in her that
she couldn't see.
Not for herself.

Every summer after
that one summer two years
ago,
my mind would
repeat the letters
of every word you ever
spoke,
my heart would knot
its chambers
and suffocate
because the baggage of
the times we spent
roamed before my eyes.

The summer that came
two years ago,
we talked about books,
music, and
hours of video chat
always seemed like
seconds.

I remember,
how you spoke of that
one song
you would play
for the person you
held close.

And here I am,
two summers later
with the same song on a
loop because
I can only let
music know
that,
I could
never become that
person
who you would have
played it for.

The summer that came
two years ago,
you found a sister in me.
While I was
at my sister's house
talking about
colleges and courses
with you.

Make me forget that summer,
will you?
because it
rose ~~my~~ our hopes for happiness
to the sky;
only to stir a
tornado of
trauma
~~I~~ we would
be swept away in.

How could I forget?
when you asked-
'let's go swimming?'
and I said
'I am scared'
because the last
time I tried to
swim,
my heart drowned;
and I lost it somewhere
to the chlorine
filled pools
that itched my eyes.

But, you said
we could find
it together,
when together
was never meant
for us.

The summer that
came two years ago,
I was busy smelling
fresh linens of
potpourri because it
reminded me of
you.
And listened
to your version
of Moonlight Sonata 14.

The summer which
came two years ago,
was just
a
recipe
to
a
disaster
because,
I used to wake
up with a smile
on my face,
with crinkles forming
at the end of my cheek.
And now,
the more I try
to smile,
the more I realize
I ~~won't~~ can't.

I don't understand
how much did it take
to taste this
kind of
freedom.
Yet, it clearly
made me want to
lurk into a
corner that I
saw in my nightmares
only to curl up
and die.

Here I am
two summers later,
my pupils dilated ~~again~~
but this time you
weren't around.
It was just the
warmth
I saved,
while I thought of you.

And here I am,
two summers later
when it is July and
a fortnight away
from your birthday.
But,
I won't be the one
who you celebrate it
with anymore.

Here I am two summers later,
in July
and it hasn't rained.
~~Not yet.~~
Maybe it
didn't rain
(on me),
because you
didn't cry
for me.
~~Not yet.~~

13. THEY SMILED..

Her skin turned bright red when
he held her in his arms.
Perhaps,
the very first time
he had held a child
was his child.

Camera shuttered while
sets of teeth popped out,
and
the mother sent a weary smile,
the grandparents had
gratitude that washed over;
aunts, uncles, brothers
and sisters
they looked happy.

They were happy,
because
I was born.
They were happy,
because
for that day
I became a reason
for people
smile,
even if they smiled
so rarely.

14. GOODBYES.

I could question
anything
but goodbyes
because,
some goodbyes
tickled the nape of
my neck.
While,
some choked it
until I was out
of air, to breathe.

Twisted and turned paths
of my life
could not swallow the
loss of their
last goodbyes.

Even though they were
long gone,
I tiptoed to those
memories
that I remember
ever so faintly
or ever so
in detail.
but,
I remember and
I always will.

I never understood,
how those moments
went by in a flash,
before my lash could
meet my eyes.

But,
we could never understand
that goodbyes aren't
a last hug,
a last word,
or a last wish.
Sometimes,
for me at least,
goodbyes were told
when I felt the
time stop-
while we were in that
moment;
having not
a care in the world
and smiling ever so
happily.

Goodbyes were told to
me-
when I wished
for the time
to last long.
For them to
last long.

108... *Alankrutha M*

The memories
of the goodbyes
or of them
always blanketed
my eyes
with the thickest
haze.

Every sight of earthen
pitchers and pots
reminded me of the time
when I said goodbye to
the crisped-up clay pot
cooked meals
and the mud beneath
where she hid ginger.

For goodbyes never came easily,
when I saw
his mouth agape,
eyes brimming with tears,
that couldn't
measure his sadness.
My eyes wouldn't
look his way that day
because
I boxed my feelings
and let it melt
into the shadows.

But the hard
goodbyes
were always the ones

I said.
Because,
Deep down the cells
I never meant
for them
To leave.
I never meant
for them to
leave me.

The harder ones
were always,
"You will not hear from
me ever again."
even if I said so
I would appear
in their dreams
to beg them and for a
million lives to
destroy me in the same way.

Perhaps,
amidst all this
the hardest goodbyes
I ever bid
was to the seasons,
even if occurred
now and then
seasons never came alone
they always brought
a bundle of
feelings,
memories,

and last of all
goodbyes.

And as summer danced
in my hair;
not for the last time
*but for the last time
at that moment.*

Deep down I knew
my hardest goodbyes
were definitely
for the seasons
because
*even if they would
come again,
nothing
would ever be the
same again.*

AUTUMN

She didn't have much to say about autumn. She was a fresh green leaf. But, then she became a crisp golden leaf, that fell to the earth because that was her place. She belonged to the ground.

1. AN OLD TURKISH BOX.

The sun beamed on the seabed,
as he traced his fingers on the book, he had just read.
Coarse crystals of sand clung to him just like in his past;
which he reckoned wouldn't last.

There sat an old Turkish box,
which had the ashes of her corpse.
Her skin, bone, and smile had melted into grey ashes.
He never tried to tear his lashes.
"Always" she used to say.
He threw the bygone box to the sea with all his might,
"Always," he said, and sure, it seemed right.

I remember the day I died inside,
the clouds fought a war in the sky.
I felt a collapse under my skin
Perhaps, a floodtide.

All I could hear was their footsteps
fading away from the face of my earth.
My wire-like shins and coat hanger shoulders
bore the decomposition from roots.

They were no longer the people who
I found at the edge of darkness,
as they lent me a pretty atlas and never
showed me the way back home.

I still remember that day-
My hair was a disheveled mess;
dripping a calamity of loneliness.
While,
They quoted a phrase that I didn't tell
Sung a song that we never wrote.

I cannot forget that day
How the phoenix eyes on my
creased fingers had worn out,
While I begged them to stay.

And that day,
Our friendship became nothing
But a long-gone fantasy.
"It is for this lifetime", they said.
Yet,
We drifted away like
Those tectonic plates.

I remember that day,
When they made me realize
That
I
Was
Lonely
Again.
Yet again.

3. HOW TO FIX A BROKEN HEART.

I was weaving a basket that day;
made of wooden splints and a cane
while I wove,
I asked my heart
"How does one fix you when you're broken?"
I remember,
how the color drained off her face.
Her crimson flush became,
the palest shade I knew.

She smiled,
but she had a face ladened with deep sorrow.
Clueless, she was.
"Could I nail your broken parts together?" I asked.
"That would draw more blood," she answered.

I let my fingers feel the rigidness of the basket;
and after a while
I said,
"Well, I could glue them with adhesives,"
"I'm afraid they have toxins," my heart said as she shrugged.

While I tried my best to knot the splints,
"Could I tie the broken parts like bookends?" I asked.
"But that would suffocate me, wouldn't it?" she said,
rather smugly-
and before I uttered another question,

she had eyes,
brimming with tears.
"Stitch me up," she said
"That would leave a scar," I said, loud.
"Could you weave a basket without getting a splinter?" she
asked, louder.

Her brows
drawn up to the inner corners,
"No," I said plainly
"Exactly!" she shrieked
"Splinter hurts made you beautiful baskets," she said.

She took a breath for what seemed
like the hundredth time
and continued
*"Scars that stitches leave would
remind me of strength,"* she spoke.

Her voice is so feeble,
her eyes are so soft
*"and strength would tell the tale of how
we survived and fixed ourselves,"*
she said.

⁂

Perhaps,
I had been feeling
the seasons under
my skin so much
that, sometimes
I forgot to
the moments it threw.

I was living for the seasons,
so much so that
I needed it to rain
to remind me of those
times when I bubbled
with curiosity and asked,
my grandma
"How do thunder and lightning occur?"
she said-
that gods fought a battle in the sky.

And now, it all came
to me
because I cared
so much about
flowers, fruits, leaves, and snowflakes
than I cared
or remembered about my own life.

By this time,
the back of my brain
tapped the corners
of my heart
which signaled that
winter was only
a few days away.

Perhaps
I had been feeling the
seasons under my skin;
because
for a fact,
Autumn was going quickly
with winter waiting
to love me.

5. THE COLONEL'S EVENING.

Yet it was the end of another day,
As the sun descended and
painted tangerine hues across the sky,
Specks of dust on the crust were
immersed in blood and gore.
The colonel scrutinized with an ivory mug in his hand
Faces dear to him were chunks of flesh that decayed.
As his mind leaped, he comprehended that,
The war is with the unison and perhaps;
for the unity.
But it seized every bit of peace and
shackled hearts in the darkest dungeons.

'War was always for the worse' he chanted,
As he knew that solace was a detached fantasy
And tranquility was a long-lost friend.

The colonel grabbed his ink and thin letterpapers
Scribbled-
futile yet aching condolences to
the bravest families of the martyrs.

War may be devoid of tranquility but, his words were not.

He wrote those letters as he was aware

That peace was not found but lent.

Unity did not exist rather, it was sacrificed.

6. DELILAH.

Lillies in my hand and a lolly in your mouth faded away.

Incandescence of your being burned into grey ashes.

Little sister, she was to me. I played with her free

Aromatic pine gardens where we laughed. You were a small girl, and you got your head smashed.

Heaven of the skies or haven of my heart, where are you, little Lilah? Don't make me cry for you again, Delilah.

7. AN OPEN DOOR.

Leave the door open, will you?
It isn't just her who yearns
for his presence.

Whether it be the rugged foot rug,
or the key stand which has their
initials engraved.
It's not only her, but even their pet awaits
with rheumy eyes while they
lifelessly lay with one another.

The couch missed him while
they lay entwined.
The kitchen missed him while
he made a mess.

He doesn't know, does he?
It's not only her heart or body that craves for him
It's an entire home.

Leave the door open, will you?
So that if he ought to pass by;
the air that caressed him
would at least enter their home and
kiss her skin
because he doesn't anymore.

❖

A coarse autumn tree without leaves
stood in sadness,
But didn't spring emerge and wash
away from the madness?

The fierce phoenix transformed into ashes.
Nonetheless, didn't it rise along with its senses?

So were the grey clouds heavy and dull;
Yet a couple of raindrops and
rays of seeping sunshine made the rainbow full.

Do remember the same love,
that one day life will be as free as that of a dove.

Consumed anger and pain,
May you let it out like rain.

Do remember the same love,
Nothing is permanent.
Neither your pain nor your struggle is reminent.

9. ONE FALL NIGHT.

It was a fall night,
As the mother tucked her daughter in her bed tight.
The little girl asked her mum for a bedtime story,
She hoped for a better trope than a king's glory.
Smoothening and stroking the girl's hair
Mum began-

"There once was a boy and a girl,
Mix tapes and thin mints for which they both twirl
And they loved each other,
So they their wedding couldn't say never.

His passion for music was vast,
So she told him she'd be his lyrics till the last.
When rain drummed on the roof,
their melodies melted into tight embraces,
which brought love to the surface.

But, through the years,
All that was left was saline tears.
Invisible walls were built between the two,
They didn't love like they did, and yes it was true.
Smiles became stardust,
Because he ran his hands on her to rust.
Vvermouth was her newfound friend,
Mixtapes and Thin Mints came to an end.

Invisible walls of silence and rage,
That was the cue for them to turn the page.

He was a wonderful guy,
There's nothing about it to lie
But invisible walls have been built,
And they aren't as fragile as a quilt. "

The mother glanced at her child asleep and crept out;
The girl did know it was about her parents without a doubt.

128... *Alankrutha M*

10. THE HARD WAY.

What does autumn do to me?
because
I caught myself pondering about faces-
that I am sure I would never see again.
Conversations with them ring bells in my ears.
When all I want is to be deaf
to them.
Deaf to the world.

"Autumn doesn't do much,"
Oh boy, I was wrong.
Every day with that chilly, crisp air
And leaves that crunch beneath my feet
reminds me of things-
I want to forget, from the outside.
(I want to forget, from the inside)

There must be a
"Better way," or
an "easier way,"
to move on;
But the
"Harder way" is always
the one
that remains close
to me, like the muffler around my neck.
Which sometimes makes me feel warm.
And sometimes, it makes me want to strangle myself.

Autumn does too much to me;
because,
It does two things
that I don't want to do.
It reminds me of those memories.
And,
Simultaneously, it taught me to forget them.
Autumn taught me
The hard way.

------◆◆◆------

11. THE SHADE AND THE BARK.

You seep like the sun through the towering canopies.
Do you still cherish and reminisce all our memories?

You were the shade and I became the bark;
I still remember the way we whispered in the dark.

But there came a day when I was uprooted away,
you did everything else than look my way.

And when the sun blazed the next day;
My wounded soul began to pray;
hoping you will always stay.

12. BLEEDING HEARTS.

When she strolled
around the road-filled
with those fallen leaves;
she saw a bleeding heart.
A shade of red brighter
than the blood that flowed through
her veins.

She saw,
how the bleeding heart
drooped at the edge of
its stalk,
trying its very best
to not fall to the hell below.

She observed;
how the bleeding heart
looked like
her-
when she went up to her
knees begging for
forgiveness
for the mistakes she never made.

And even though,
there were those
parts in that flower
that were lashed with crimson
ink,
At the edges, she saw a shade
of pure white;
a free canvas
with no colors on it.

When she saw the bleeding heart;
the sad, sleepy heart
was not all
that the flower had.
There was an unstained pure
white,
which had begged for life
in it.

13. A DECIDIOUS LEAF.

I crunch like the leaves of the deciduous.
Fading footsteps would never admire
the gradient of my being.
Mustard or tangerine I might be
But,
They would still stamp on me.
As to them, I lay there
under their feet, and
on the concrete
like a lifeless leaf.

There was something about
the way,
how
seasons slipped to become
silt that loosened through the
gaps of her fingers.

Days went by days,
and nights melted away.
Soon,
she knew that
October eyes would
widen its arm and
pull her into winter.

There was something about
the way
how seasons slipped
because
even when she was only
a few days away
from a new season
she felt so much at ease,

There wasn't the fear which
lingered around her like
dark shadows-
that fear was gone.

While she blew her candles off,
and warmed herself to sleep
that night-
The rusty metal rods of her bed came in
contact with her bony fingers.
She had the musing of rusting
away like those metals.
She put those thoughts
into a hibernation.

The curtains of her
windows,
struggled-
to stay at a place
as and when cold air
creams onto the
walls of her bedroom, and
froze her bed.

Then slowly,
and rather
surreptitiously
it reached
her.

She could see the winter
circle her room
examining places,
where warmth subsided
and engulf those
areas that warmth
had built a home in.

Winter saw her now,
she sat up straight-
her mind burning with
all those memories
of all the seasons
that had ended.
Her breath was coarse.
She was tongue-tied.
She couldn't speak.

But she should.
(she should)
she told herself.

Winter whooshed;
it's way into the tiniest
corner of her house
except her.
(except her)
She still didn't feel
nervous
or scared.

And when winter
came and stood before her-
she asked,
why winter hadn't engulfed
her yet.

Winter said-
"I used to cloud your life
like how moss did to those
beautiful blue rivers.

I wanted to conceal
what was always meant
for the world to see.

Even though my horizon was thin,
I still wanted to know
Once,
just once how it felt
to be on the ground
because,
you have the patience
of what the earth bears
to have held a sadness
that could kill a life.

You might hate me,
or despise me
But hear me out, will you?
I would *always* come around
because,
I want you to *always* be around.

Did it ever occur to you?
that maybe
being cold would *make me feel cold
too?*
I found a source of warmth
that made me want to nuzzle
into you.

But,
even though you
hate me,

you are still standing quiet
listening to my hushed whisper.

Perhaps,
on top of all of it
you spoke of me first,
*you always spoke of winter
first.*
because,
maybe seasons started
with spring-
but to you;
(yes, to me)
I always came first-
your seasons
started with the winter.

Because,
deep down-
even though
your fragrant flowers bloomed
in the spring,
your sweet fruits beckoned
to you in summer, and
you were left with crushed
leaves and a crushed heart
in the fall.
You *always* spoke
of me,
like a bitter memory never forgotten.
You *always*
thought of me,
through all

the other seasons.

If it weren't for the
Cold,
you would've never known
the other seasons.

If it weren't for
the way you loathe me-
you wouldn't have explored.

If it weren't for me
or the way my coldness built
a fort in your heart;
you would've
never known
the
seasons
within
you."

- winter had heard her birthday wish.

❖

With all the love, that there is.
Give mine, to the seasons which made me
write this book.

The end.

Made in the USA
Monee, IL
07 July 2026

56550603R00085